ABOVE *Charles Lutwidge Dodgson (Lewis Carroll), 1857
(The Governing Body of Christ Church, Oxford).*

PREVIOUS PAGE *Alice Liddell by Charles Dodgson, 1860
(National Geographic/Getty Images).*

Lewis Carroll

Alice's Adventures Under Ground

THE ORIGINAL MANUSCRIPT

●————————— THE ORIGINAL MANUSCRIPT —————————●

THE BRITISH LIBRARY

Introduction

by Sally Brown

Describing the inspiration for his magical 'fairy-tale', *Alice's Adventures in Wonderland*, the author Charles Lutwidge Dodgson – later to be celebrated throughout the world as Lewis Carroll – wrote in 1888:

> The germ of *Alice* was an extensive story, told in a boat to the 3 children of Dean Liddell: it was afterwards, at the request of Miss Alice Liddell, written out for her, in MS [manuscript] print, with pen-and-ink pictures (*such* pictures!) of my own devising: without the least idea, at the time, that it would ever be published. But friends urged me to print it, so it was re-written, and enlarged, and published.

1 Charles Lutwidge Dodgson (sitting on the grass to the left), with his family at Croft Rectory, Yorkshire, albumen print, c.1852–60 (National Portrait Gallery, London).

Although *Alice* would become perhaps the most famous and best-loved children's tale of all time, the original story – *Alice's Adventures under Ground* – remains less well-known.

It all began one 'golden afternoon' in 1862 when Charles Dodgson, a shy young mathematics tutor at Christ Church, Oxford, accompanied Alice Liddell and her two sisters on a family boating trip. The children's parents, Henry Liddell, the new Dean of the Cathedral college, and his wife, Lorina, had arrived in 1855 with four youngsters, Harry, Lorina, Alice and Edith; four more – two girls and two boys – were to be born in Oxford.

Dodgson himself was the third child and eldest son in a family of seven girls and four boys, and had always taken pleasure in children's company. Brought up with his lively, affectionate brothers and sisters in a Yorkshire rectory (*fig.* 1), he revealed at an early age the talent for storytelling, jokes, riddles, elaborate games and entertainments which was to enthrall his 'child-friends', as he called them, throughout his life. In 1853, two years after his arrival in Oxford as an undergraduate, he began to keep a diary, a habit which continued until his death forty-five years later. Four volumes of his diaries are lost, but the nine which have survived are now in the British Library; it is through them that we are able to chart the course of the most important of these friendships, which eventually led to the writing of the 'fairytale' that was to become *Alice's Adventures in Wonderland*.

In Dodgson's diary entry for 6 March 1856 we find the first mention of his having made the acquaintance of 'little Harry Liddell … certainly the handsomest boy I ever saw'. Two days later he relates that, at a musical party in the Deanery, he 'took the opportunity of making friends with Lorina'. It was not until the following term, however, that he met Alice, who was then just under four years old, and the smallest sister, Edith. On 25 April 1856 he went with his friend Reginald Southey to the Deanery, to try – with a borrowed camera – to take a photograph of the Cathedral. Two attempts to do so were unsuccessful, but his diary continues: 'The three little girls were in the garden most of the time, and we became excellent friends: we tried to group them in the foreground of the picture, but they were not patient sitters.' The entry concludes with the significant pronouncement, 'I mark this day with a white stone'; this, the Roman poet Catullus' symbol for a day of good fortune, was reserved by Dodgson for particularly memorable occasions.

Dodgson and Southey returned to the Deanery on three successive days during the following week, and succeeded in taking more photographs of the Liddell children, despite great difficulty in getting them to sit still. A few days later, Dodgson proudly took a 'fair profile' of Harry to the Deanery and was invited to stay to lunch. The Dean, himself a photography enthusiast, was impressed with Dodgson's work and this occasion marked the beginning of a period of frequent comings and goings between the shy, stuttering don and the lively, intelligent young Liddells. As the friendship grew, photography sessions were interspersed with croquet, puppet shows and plays, conjuring performances, long walks and river picnics.

When collodion wet-plate photography became available to the public in 1855, Dodgson, who had been interested in drawing and painting from his youth, was immediately attracted to this new art form. Despite experimenting with varied subjects, including landscapes and architecture, his most successful photographs were of children – especially little girls, in whose company his habitual stammer would 'softly and suddenly vanish away' like the subject of his famous poem, *The Hunting of the Snark*. The fact that he is now acclaimed as one of the most successful and imaginative Victorian photographers is due not merely to his technical skills but his natural ability to charm and entertain his sitters. He first photographed the Liddell children with his own camera on 3 June 1856. Many years later, in 1932, Alice recalled that she and her sisters never resented having to sit still for a long time as he took their photograph, because of the wonderful stories he would tell them as he did so, 'illustrating them by pencil and ink drawings as he went along'. 'When we were thoroughly happy and amused at his stories,' she wrote, 'he used to pose us, and expose the plates, before the right

2 *Edith, Lorina and Alice Liddell by Charles Dodgson, albumen print*, 1858 (*National Portrait Gallery, London*).

mood had passed [*fig. 2*]. He seemed to have an endless fund of fantastical stories, which he made up as he told them ...'

Dodgson's photographic skills soon began to attract admirers in Oxford and further afield. Queen Victoria's son, the Prince of Wales, who was an undergraduate at Christ Church during this period, singled out his portrayal of Lorina and Alice dressed as Chinamen for particular praise; the Poet Laureate, Alfred Tennyson, was so entranced by a photograph of Alice posing as a ragged beggar girl (*fig.* 3) that he declared it the most beautiful portrait of a child he had ever seen. From the first, Alice was Dodgson's favourite, and his photographs of her possess a special, almost haunting quality. She was a charming and very pretty child with short, straight dark hair cut in a fringe, large blue eyes

3 *Alice Liddell dressed as a beggar girl by Dodgson,*
hand-coloured photograph, c.1858
(Mr Douglas Smith).

and a strikingly gentle and innocent face; in later years Dodgson always preferred to remember her as 'an entirely fascinating seven-year-old maiden'. Like the heroine of her 'adventures', she was full of intelligent curiosity, and loved reading. Of the many photographs of her on her own, one of the most simple and successful shows her in pensive profile, sitting on a high-backed wooden chair (*fig*. 4). Dodgson was constantly thinking of new ideas to please her, summoning up his best stories, puzzles and jokes, and was desolate on the rare occasions when she did not respond with her usual cheerfulness and enthusiasm. In a letter of February 1861 to his sister Mary, he reports, 'My small friends the Liddells are all in the measles just now. I met them yesterday. Alice ... looked awfully melancholy – it was almost impossible to make her smile ...' Alice herself recalled in old age the happy days she and her sisters spent in Dodgson's company: 'One of our favourite whole-day excursions was to row down to Nuneham and picnic in the woods there ... Sometimes we were told stories after luncheon that transported us into Fairyland ...'

Nuneham, with its landscaped park and deep, mysterious woods, provided the ideal destination for a day's outing. Five miles downstream from Oxford, it was just the right distance away and in the easiest direction for the children to row. In her reminiscences, Alice described their rowing lessons in some detail: 'Mr Dodgson ... succeeded in teaching us in the course of these excursions, and it proved an unending joy ... It was a proud day when we could "feather our oars" properly.'

Dodgson himself captures his delight in these river trips, and the children's eager attempts at rowing, in the first stanza of the prefatory poem to *Alice's Adventures in Wonderland*:

> All in the golden afternoon
> Full leisurely we glide;
> For both our oars, with little skill,
> By little arms are plied,
> While little hands make vain pretence
> Our wanderings to guide.

On 4 July 1862, a fine summer's day, the three girls – then thirteen, ten and eight years old – set out with Dodgson on an expedition, which was destined to make literary history. They left the Deanery after lunch, dressed as usual in white cotton dresses, wide brimmed hats, white socks and black buttoned shoes. Their governess, the formidably named Miss Prickett, walked with them as far as Dodgson's rooms in the Old Library, and left them there in the care of Dodgson and his friend Robinson Duckworth, a Fellow of Trinity College; the children were greatly taken with his charm, sense of humour and fine singing voice. With the men carrying the picnic baskets, the party made its way through Christ Church Meadow to Folly Bridge, where they chose their boat and set off upstream for a change. Dodgson's diary entry records: 'Duckworth and I made an expedition *up* the river to Godstow with the 3 Liddells: we had tea on the bank there, and did not reach Christ Church again until ½ past 8 …' On the opposite page is a later note dated 10 February 1863: 'On which occasion I told them the fairy-tale of "Alice's Adventures under Ground", which I undertook to write out for Alice, and which is now finished …' Duckworth later recalled this momentous day:

> I rowed *stroke* and he rowed *bow* in the famous Long Vacation voyage to Godstow, when the three Miss Liddells were our passengers, and the story was actually composed and spoken *over my shoulder* for the benefit of Alice Liddell, who was acting as 'cox' of our gig. I remember turning round and saying, 'Dodgson, is this an *extempore* romance of yours?' And he replied, 'Yes, I'm inventing as we go along.'

Duckworth also remembered Alice begging his friend, on the children's return to the Deanery, to write out this particularly enthralling story for her, and Dodgson's claim that he had then stayed up nearly all night, 'committing to a MS book his recollections of the drolleries with which he had enlivened the afternoon'.

Whether or not Dodgson actually worked for most of that night, as Duckworth declared, his diary for the next day records that on the

4 A profile portrait of Alice Liddell
by Dodgson, sepia photograph, 1859
(Mr Douglas Smith).

train up to London, where he was going to see the 1862 Exhibition, he wrote out the 'headings' of *Alice's Adventures under Ground*.

Twenty-five years later, in an article for *The Theatre*, he described the 'golden afternoon' that inspired the famous tale: '... the cloudless blue above, the watery mirror below, the boat drifting idly on its way, the tinkle of the drops that fell from the oars, as they waved so sleepily to and fro, and … the three eager faces…from whose lips "Tell us a story, please" had all the stern immutability of Fate!' He also recalled that, 'in a desperate attempt to strike out some new line of fairy-lore', he had sent Alice 'straight down a rabbit-hole, to begin with, without the least idea what was to happen afterwards'. Many of the subsequent happenings were, in fact, inspired by particular Oxford events, characters and situations which, though strongly tinged with fantasy, would have been instantly recognisable to the children. Alice later recalled that her 'frequent interruptions' would open up 'fresh and undreamed of possibilities' as the story progressed.

In early August 1862, Dodgson took the children on another trip to Godstow, during which, he wrote in his diary, 'I had to go on with my interminable fairy-tale of *Alice's Adventures*.' On the Liddell family's return from their annual seaside holiday, however, his meetings with the three sisters became less frequent. Mrs Liddell may have felt that his friendship with her daughters was becoming too close; when he came across Lorina, Alice and Edith in the college quadrangle on 13 November, he commented in his diary that this was 'a rare event of late'. Perhaps Alice reminded him of his promise to write down her 'adventures' on this occasion, for the entry continues: 'Began writing the fairy-tale for Alice, which I told them July 4th, going to Godstow – I hope to finish it by Christmas.' By this he presumably means the formal manuscript he was preparing, since the 'headings' and rough notes were already in existence. He had finished writing this out in his neat 'manuscript print' hand, using sepia-coloured ink, by February 1863, but it took him much longer to complete the 'pen and ink pictures … of my own devising' with which he had decided to embellish it.

In fact, 1863 was to be the last year in which Dodgson continued to see Alice with any regularity. In March he received a letter from her in French, asking him to accompany her to the grand and elaborate 'illuminations' held in Oxford to celebrate the marriage of the Prince of Wales and Princess Alexandra (a 'white stone' day); in April he joined the Liddell children on a visit to their grandmother, who lived near Cheltenham; in May he presented Alice with a book as an eleventh birthday present; in June there were more river picnics (now, however, with Miss Prickett in attendance), the exciting preparations for the visit to Christ Church of the newly wed Prince and Princess, a bazaar, and a trip to the circus. On 25 June Dodgson joined a large Liddell family river outing to Nuneham which ended in his taking Alice and her sisters back to Oxford by train: 'a pleasant expedition,' he wrote in his diary, 'with a very pleasant conclusion'.

Immediately after this episode, a crisis occurred in Dodgson's relations with the family, causing a break with the Dean and Mrs Liddell and cutting him off from the children for some months. We do not know the precise nature of this crisis because, many years later, Dodgson's niece, Menella, cut out the page of his diary containing entries for 27, 28 and 29 June. Some surviving notes made by her suggest that it might have arisen from Oxford gossip about Dodgson's paying too much attention to Lorina, now rapidly developing into a beautiful young woman. Clearly, he was deeply upset and offended by whatever had occurred between him and the Liddells, for on 2 December he wrote in his diary that he had seen the children with their mother, 'but I held aloof from them, as I have done all this term'. Even before this rift arose, however, it was plain that Mrs Liddell, who had high social ambitions for her daughters, did not always welcome Dodgson's friendship with them. Although the atmosphere gradually thawed, his relationship with Alice and her sisters never returned to its former ease and closeness; by May 1865, he was sufficiently estranged from Alice to comment after a chance meeting that she had 'changed a good deal, and hardly for the better'.

The manuscript of *Alice's Adventures under Ground* was finally despatched to Alice as an early Christmas present, on 26 November 1864. It was bound as a little book of ninety pages, in dark morocco leather, with a beautifully designed and coloured title page and the slightly wistful dedication, 'To a dear child, in memory of a summer day'. The thirty-seven illustrations – fourteen of them full-page – had taken a long time to complete, and caused Dodgson, who was completely untrained as an artist, a certain amount of anguish. He borrowed a natural history book from the Deanery to help with the

animal subjects, and took infinite trouble with many trial sketches.
Some of the comic drawings in the manuscript (for instance, those
illustrating 'You are old, Father William', a parody of a poem by
Robert Southey) are reminiscent of Edward Lear, whose *Book of
Nonsense* was published in 1846; they also recall Dodgson's lively
childhood sketches for the family magazines, with such titles as *The
Rectory Umbrella* and *Mischmasch*, which he wrote for the amusement
of his siblings. Several of his illustrations of the long-haired Alice (he
had decided that the story's heroine should not physically resemble his
'ideal child-friend') possess a distinctly Pre-Raphaelite quality: the full-
page illustration of a magically expanded Alice trapped in the White
Rabbit's house, for instance, was inspired by a Dante Gabriel Rossetti
print, and her pose, with head inclined, holding the 'little magic
bottle' was taken from Arthur Hughes's painting *The Lady with the
Lilacs*, which Dodgson owned (*fig.* 5). He was a great admirer of
this group of artists, and had photographed several of them. At the
very end of his little book, Dodgson made a small head-and-shoulders
drawing of the 'real' Alice at the age of seven, carefully copied from a
photograph (*see* p.1). This charming image is, in fact, his only surviving
drawing of her, but he must have been dissatisfied with it because he
then pasted the oval photograph on top. The original sketch beneath
was not discovered until 1977, by the Canadian scholar (and now
Dodgson's biographer) Morton Cohen. An ingenious paper hinge
now allows the two images to be seen one on top of the other.

When Dodgson had finished writing out the text of *Alice's
Adventures under Ground* he lent it to a friend, the children's novelist
George MacDonald, whose opinion he trusted, and whose 1858
fairy-tale, *Phantastes*, he particularly admired. Mrs MacDonald read it
aloud to her children, to their great delight. Dodgson's diary entry
for 9 May 1863 includes the announcement that 'They wish me to
publish.' Once the finished manuscript was installed at the Deanery,
where visitors were invited to admire it, Henry Kingsley, novelist
brother of the author of *The Water Babies*, was so taken with the
story that he insisted that Mrs Liddell urge Dodgson to consider its
publication. By this time, however, the process was already underway.
Dodgson later wrote that 'there was no idea of publication in my

5 The Lady with the Lilacs *by Arthur Hughes, oil, 1863*
*(Art Gallery of Ontario, Toronto, Canada/Presented in
memory of Frances Baines, 1966/The Bridgeman Art Library).*

mind when I wrote this little book; *that* was wholly an afterthought, pressed on me by the "perhaps too partial friends" who always have to bear the blame when an author rushes into print.'

As soon as he began to contemplate publication, Dodgson realised that the original story would have to be fleshed out with more incidents and characters. Some of the private Liddell family jokes and references were removed, as was the lyrical passage at the very end of the story which describes 'an ancient city, and a quiet river winding near it along the plain'. As he later explained, the first, more private version of Alice's adventures was 're-written, and enlarged', eventually growing from eighteen thousand to thirty-five thousand words; two completely new chapters, 'Pig and Pepper' and 'A Mad Tea-Party', were added, and the final trial scene was greatly expanded to incorporate some of the new characters, including the Hatter, with his companions the March Hare and the Dormouse, and the Duchess's fierce, pepper-dispensing cook.

Despite these changes and additions, however, many allusions to people and places that were familiar to Alice and her sisters remain embedded in the published story. The three little girls in the Dormouse's rambling account of the 'treacle well', Elsie, Lacie and Tillie, are the three Liddells in disguise: Elsie stands for L.C., the initials of Lorina Charlotte; Lacie is an anagram of Alice; and Matilda ('Tillie') was a family nickname for Edith. The lessons described by the Mock Turtle and Gryphon are a joking allusion to the children's experiences at the hands of Miss Prickett and several other masters and mistresses who tried to teach them 'extras', including the Quadrille, transformed in Dodgson's version into a solemn dance of sea creatures. The poem 'Twinkle twinkle little bat' is thought to refer to Professor Bartholomew Price, whom the children nicknamed 'Bat', and the inspiration for the Hatter is alleged to have been Theophilus Carter, an eccentric Oxford furniture dealer.

Although he had used local presses for printing small pamphlets, Dodgson now needed a proper London publisher, and found one in Alexander Macmillan, introduced to him by an Oxford friend in October 1863. Macmillan was delighted by the story, and the two men entered into a commission agreement: Dodgson would bear the expenses of publishing his book and Macmillan would receive a percentage of the gross profits for producing and distributing it. During the course of its production they established a close working relationship. Dodgson bombarded Macmillan with letters about every aspect of the book; on 11 November 1864, for instance, he declared: 'I have been considering the question of the *colour* of *Alice's Adventures* and have come to the conclusion that *bright red* will be the best – not the best, perhaps, artistically, but the most attractive to childish eyes.'

Once he had settled on a publisher, Dodgson's next step – having decided, rather reluctantly, that his own drawings were not professional enough – was to find an illustrator. Duckworth suggested John Tenniel, an acclaimed artist, whose work appeared regularly in the comic magazine *Punch*, which Dodgson enjoyed reading. On 20 December 1863, two months after his first meeting with Macmillan, he wrote to his friend Tom Taylor, a dramatist and critic (and later editor of *Punch*), asking him if he knew Tenniel well enough 'to say whether he could undertake such a thing as drawing a dozen woodcuts to illustrate a child's book'.

A month later, armed with Taylor's letter of introduction, Dodgson called on Tenniel in London. He found the artist 'receptive' to the idea of 'undertaking the pictures', though he delayed his final decision until he had seen the manuscript. Tenniel was invited to Oxford to explore the background to the story, the familiar scenes and objects which Dodgson had, consciously or unconsciously, woven into his fantastic tale of Alice's encounters with a variety of strange creatures and situations 'under ground'. Dodgson's diary entry for 12 October 1864 describes the early stages of their relationship, which was dogged by delays on Tenniel's part, often caused by the ceaseless weekly demands of *Punch*: 'Called on Macmillan and had some talk about the book ... Thence I went to Tenniel's, who showed me one drawing on wood ... of Alice sitting by the pool of tears, and the rabbit hurrying away. We discussed the book, and agreed on about 34 pictures ...' Tenniel eventually produced seven more than this projected figure.

Some of Tenniel's illustrations in *Alice's Adventures in Wonderland* are clearly based on Dodgson's original drawings (Alice swimming in the pool of tears, for instance), but when he came to the new characters and episodes which appeared in the expanded story, he

*6 Alice chats to the Duchess, Alice's Adventures in Wonderland,
illustrated by John Tenniel, 1866 (BL, C.59.g.11, f.132).*

had more of a free hand. His drawings of the Hatter, March Hare, Dormouse, grinning Cheshire cat and fierce Duchess, are brilliantly witty and accomplished (*fig.* 6). Alice herself, with her perfectly composed china doll features, has a far more grown-up air in Tenniel's illustrations than in Dodgson's occasionally awkward drawings of his seven-year-old heroine.

Dodgson's extreme perfectionism could make working with him, at times, a distinctly wearying experience. Christ Church Library still possesses his elaborate plan of the illustrations for the published book; several of his own designs for the title page; his carefully corrected proof pages; and his own undulating, pasted mock-up of the entirely new 'Mouse's Tail' poem (more overtly threatening in tone than the simple rhyme of the first version). The exchanges between author and illustrator are not well documented; Tenniel probably destroyed Dodgson's letters and only a few brief notes from artist to author have survived. In the end, it was a mutual obsession with detail which helped to calm the occasional outbursts of anger and pique which arose throughout their collaboration. There can be no doubt, however, about the success of Tenniel's contribution to the published book; the peculiar charm of the story and its vivid, entrancing images is for most readers inseparable from his illustrations, which were expertly carved into woodblocks (now on permanent loan to the British Library) by the famous Dalziel brothers.

The British Library possesses a letter from Dodgson to Tom Taylor, dated 10 June 1864, in which he asks for help in 'fixing on a name for my fairy-tale'. He had decided that the original title was not sufficiently mysterious, enticing or magical. Several possibilities are listed: 'Alice among the Elves/Goblins', 'Alice's Hour in Elfland' and 'Alice's Hour/Adventures in Wonderland', which Taylor liked best.

The first edition of *Alice's Adventures in Wonderland* appeared at long last at the end of June 1865, under the pseudonym 'Lewis Carroll' (an adaptation of his first two names), which Dodgson had used before in sending contributions to comic magazines. Two thousand copies were printed by the Clarendon Press; Dodgson inscribed 'twenty or more' as 'presents to various friends' and sent a special copy bound in white vellum to Alice at the Deanery, to mark the third anniversary of their famous river journey.

One of the few surviving copies of the first printing is preserved at the British Library. It is now known as the 'suppressed edition'. Tenniel had felt 'entirely dissatisfied with the printing of the pictures', as he wrote to Dodgson on 19 July. Nine of his illustrations appeared to be printed a little lighter, and another nine a little heavier, than he thought desirable. With some anguish, Dodgson decided that all existing copies should be withdrawn. In cancelling the edition, he stood to lose a substantial amount of his own money; altogether, he had spent a total of £497 on the book (almost Tenniel's annual *Punch* salary), of which the artist received £138, the Dalziels £142 for their engravings, the printers £137 and the binders and advertisers £80. Nevertheless, he refused to compromise on its artistic quality, and respected Tenniel's objections.

Dodgson felt compelled to write to those friends who had already received copies to ask for their return, 'as the pictures are so badly done'. He engaged a new printer, Richard Clay of London, and the first copy of the new impression, although dated 1866, arrived at Christ Church on 9 November 1865. Tenniel kept him waiting almost a month before expressing his approval, at which point Dodgson felt free at last to praise the book; he declared in his diary that it was 'very *far* superior to the old, and in fact a perfect piece of artistic printing'. The imperfect first edition was sold, at Tenniel's suggestion, to America, where it was issued by Appleton of New York. Little did he or Tenniel imagine that the few surviving English copies of the 'suppressed' edition would one day command huge sums of money and be fought over by book collectors.

Alice's Adventures in Wonderland was widely reviewed and received almost unconditional praise. Dodgson kept a careful record in his diary of the early notices. *The Reader* described it as 'a glorious artistic treasure', while the *Press* admired its 'simple and attractive style', judged it 'amusingly written' and declared that 'a child, when once the tale has commenced, will long to hear the whole of this wondrous narrative'. The *Publisher's Circular* selected it as 'the most original and the most charming' of the children's books sent to them that year, the *Bookseller* announced that 'a more original fairy tale ... it has not lately been our good fortune to read', and the *Guardian* thought it 'graceful' and 'full of humour'. Only the *Athenaeum* struck a different note: 'We fear that any child might be more puzzled than enchanted by this stiff, overwrought story.'

Sales of the book began steadily, and then rapidly increased. New editions appeared annually from 1866–8, Dodgson receiving a handsome profit of £250 after just two years. From 1869–89 a series of twenty-six reprinted editions were issued, each one carefully supervised by Dodgson and, where the illustrations were concerned, by Tenniel. As the audience of admirers widened, many translations into other languages followed, several of these also overseen by the author. The witty, challenging text, filled with puns, literary jokes and parodies of such famous poets as Southey and Wordsworth, appealed to adults as well as children. Christina Rossetti wrote to offer Dodgson 'a thousand and one thanks ... for the funny pretty book you have so very kindly sent me. My Mother and Sister as well as myself made ourselves quite at home yesterday in Wonderland: and ... I confess it would give me sincere pleasure to fall in with that conversational rabbit, that endearing puppy, that very sparkling dormouse ... The woodcuts are charming.' Her brother, Dante Gabriel Rossetti, commented that 'The wonderful ballad of Father William and Alice's perverted snatches of school poetry are among the funniest things I have seen for a long while.' (*fig. 7*) The book's admirers included Queen Victoria herself; the legend persists that, having read it with great enjoyment, she asked that the author's next work should be sent to her and was not amused when this turned out to be a geometry textbook entitled *An Elementary Treatise on Determinants*.

The cherished image of the 'real' Alice remained with Dodgson for the rest of his life. Throughout his later years, and despite numerous new 'childfriends', his greatest consolation was to summon up the memory of the 'happy summer days' spent with her and her sisters. One of their last meetings took place on 25 June 1870, when Alice was eighteen years old. Mrs Liddell brought her, with Lorina, to be photographed in Dodgson's new set of college rooms. The photograph of Alice shows a solemn, unsmiling young woman, formally dressed, her hair neatly pinned up, staring rather bleakly into the camera lens – a striking contrast to the charming, eager, animated little girl in the portraits taken ten years earlier (*fig.* 8).

A year later, on 4 May 1871, Dodgson wrote in his diary: 'On … Alice's birthday, I sit down to record the events of the day, partly as a specimen of my life now …'. In December of that year his sequel to *Wonderland*, entitled *Through the Looking-Glass, and What Alice Found There* (once again illustrated by Tenniel), was published, and the first thing Dodgson did when he received his advance copies was to send

7 The Rossettis, Dante Gabriel, Christina, Frances and William, by Dodgson, 1863 (Time & Life Pictures/Getty Images).

8 Dodgson's last photograph of Alice, 1870
(Mr Douglas Smith).

three over to the Deanery, 'the one for Alice being in morocco'. The new story, describing Alice's adventures as she moves symbolically from child to adult in another magical world entered through the mirror in her Oxford drawing-room, drew together many anecdotes, events and ideas from different points in its author's life: the framework of a living chess game, for instance, probably makes use of private jokes and incidents from the days when Dodgson was teaching the Liddell children to play chess (*fig.* 9); the ideas based on mirror reversal – the White Queen's 'backward' memory, Alice's puzzlement at the notion that she has to walk away from an object in order to go towards it – arise from his fascination with logical inversion.

9 Alice and the Red Queen, Through the Looking-Glass, and
What Alice Found There ... *illustrated by John Tenniel, 1872*
(BL, C.71.b.33, f.35).

Other publications by 'Lewis Carroll' appeared during the
period when Dodgson was preparing *Through the Looking Glass*
for publication. Shortly after his return from his only trip abroad,
an expedition to Russia with a Christ Church colleague in the
summer of 1867, his fairy story 'Bruno's Revenge' was published
in the popular children's periodical *Aunt Judy's Magazine.*
Phantasmagoria, his first book of collected verse – containing both
comic and serious poems – appeared in 1869, and a collection of his

Oxford pamphlets came out, under his real name, in 1874, the same year as the long, mysterious nonsense poem *The Hunting of the Snark*. A retelling of the *Wonderland* story, in a shortened and simplified version for children below the age of five, entitled *The Nursery Alice*, was published in 1889 (*fig*. 10).

Meanwhile, in the summer of 1880, when Alice was twenty-eight, she was married in Westminster Abbey to Reginald Hargreaves, the only son of a wealthy mill owner and property magnate from Lancashire, who had been been educated at Eton and Christ Church. Five years after her marriage, Dodgson wrote to 'Alice-Liddell-that-was', as he described her in his diary. The letter began, 'I fancy this will come to you almost like a voice from the dead, after so many years of silence, but my mental picture is still as vivid as ever of one who was, through so many years, my ideal child-friend.' It went on to ask 'whether you have any objection to the original manuscript book of Alice's Adventures (which I suppose you still possess) being published in facsimile? ... I think, considering the extraordinary popularity the books have had (we have sold more than 120,000 of the two), there must be many who would like to see the original form.'

Alice consented to this request, and sent him her treasured manuscript. Dodgson wrote five more times in the next twenty months, reporting the progress of the facsimile and discussing various details concerning the preface and the use of the profits, which he suggested should go to a children's hospital. The book appeared as *Alice's Adventures under Ground* in 1886; Alice received a copy inscribed 'To Her, whose namesake one happy summer day inspired his story: from the Author, Xmas 1886'.

Dodgson died twelve years later, on 14 January 1898, of a sudden attack of bronchial pneumonia which struck during the Christmas holiday with his family in Guildford, while he was working hard on the second volume of his *Symbolic Logic*. He had often contemplated death and accepted its approach without fear, writing to one of his sisters in 1896: 'It is getting increasingly difficult now to remember *which* of one's friends remain alive, and *which* have gone "into the land of the great departed, into the silent land". Also, such news comes as less and less of a shock, and more and more one realises that it is an experience each of *us* has to face before long …' He left instructions that his funeral be 'simple and inexpensive, avoiding all things which are merely done for show'. Many good friends and colleagues attended it, but no members of the Liddell family. His relatives cleared his Christ Church rooms, burning many papers, letters and manuscripts, but retaining a few of his possessions for themselves. In May an auction was held of many of his beloved gadgets, games, puzzles, books, furniture, portraits, paintings and sketches, photographs, albums and cameras – all knocked down to the highest bidder.

Alice, however, continued to treasure the manuscript story of her 'adventures' until 1928 when, aged seventy-five, widowed and faced with substantial death duties, she put it up for sale at Sotheby's, in London. 'Lewis Carroll' was by now a name revered throughout the world, his manuscripts and inscribed first editions eagerly sought by rich collectors. The auction was held on 3 April, and Alice herself attended to see the little book purchased for £15,000 – a record price at that time – by an American dealer, Dr Rosenbach, who took it back with him to Philadelphia and sold it on to a wealthy collector, Eldridge Johnson, president of the Victor Talking Machine Company.

She resumed her by now rather lonely existence at Cuffnells, the Hargreaves family house in Hampshire; two of her three sons had been tragically killed in action in the Great War, and the third had moved away. In 1932, however, her life changed dramatically when, at eighty years old, she was invited to New York, to attend the lavish Lewis Carroll centenary celebrations at Columbia University, accompanied by her son Caryl and sister Rhoda. Here she was treated as a celebrity: admirers of the *Alice* books queued up to pay homage to her, she appeared in a Paramount newsreel, addressed the American people on the radio, wrote an article for the *New York Times* and received an honorary doctorate of letters. The remaining

10 The Nursery Alice *by Lewis Carroll, published by Edward
Gordon Craig, 1898–1901 (BL, Cup.410.g.4, cover).*

two years of her life were filled with new activity – answering
letters about Lewis Carroll, making public appearances, unveiling
memorials – until she was finally moved to confess to her son
that she was 'tired of being Alice in Wonderland'.

In 1946, following the death of its American owner, the original *Alice* manuscript again came up for auction, in New York. Rosenbach again bought it, this time for $50,000. A plan was then hatched, however, by the prominent bibliophile Lessing Rosenwald, who persuaded a group of wealthy benefactors that the famous little book should be returned to its own country, as a gesture of thanks for the British people's gallantry in the Second World War. On 6 November 1948 the Librarian of Congress sailed for England on the *Queen Elizabeth*, taking the manuscript with him (and occasionally sleeping with it under his pillow). On 12 November he presented it to the British Museum 'as an expression of thanks to a noble people who kept Hitler at bay for a long period single-handed'. The Archbishop of Canterbury, who accepted it on behalf of the nation, acclaimed this gesture as 'an unsullied and innocent act in a distracted and sinful world' – a sentiment which would have appealed to the story's creator.

Visitors from all over the world continue to flock to Christ Church in search of Lewis Carroll and Alice. Dodgson's sitting-room is now a graduate common room: its original appearance is preserved only in a photograph. His William de Morgan fireplace tiles, with their strange creatures reminiscent of Wonderland, have been made into a fire screen which is now in the Senior Common Room. In the Great Hall, where one of the stained-glass windows is dedicated to Dodgson and Alice, hangs a rather sombre portrait of him, painted after his death. In the Library is Alice's son Caryl Hargreaves's collection of hundreds of editions of the 'Alice' stories, in many languages, together with a fascinating hoard of 'Wonderland' and 'Looking-Glass' toys, games and memorabilia. The college also possesses a few of the 'real' Alice's possessions, some of them – gloves, fan, playing cards – strangely evocative of Dodgson's 'fairy-tale' of long ago, the original version of which is now one of the greatest treasures on display in the British Library's exhibition galleries.

Further Reading

Clark, Anne, *The Real Alice* (Michael Joseph Ltd., 1981)

Cohen, Morton N. (ed.), *The Letters of Lewis Carroll*
(Macmillan Publishers Ltd., 1979)

Cohen, Morton N., *Lewis Carroll, a Biography*
(Macmillan Publishers Ltd., 1995)

Gardner, Martin (ed.), *The Annotated Alice*
(W.W. Norton & Co., 2000)

Green, Roger Lancelyn (ed.), *The Diaries of Lewis Carroll*
(Random House, 1953)

Phillips, Robert, *Aspects of Alice* (Penguin Books, 1974)

Thomas, Donald Serrell, *Lewis Carroll: A Biography*
(Barnes & Noble, 1999)

Alice's
Adventures
under
Ground

A Christmas Gift
to
a Dear Child
in Memory
of
a Summer Day.

Chapter 1.

Alice was beginning to get very tired of sitting by her sister on the bank, and of having nothing to do: once or twice she had peeped into the book her sister was reading, but it had no pictures or conversations in it, and where is the use of a book, thought Alice, without pictures or con- -versations? So she was considering in her own mind, (as well as she could, for the hot day made her feel very sleepy and stupid,) whether the pleasure of making a daisy-chain was worth the trouble of getting up and picking the daisies, when a white rabbit with pink eyes ran close by her.

There was nothing very remarkable in that, nor did Alice think it so very much out of the way to hear the rabbit say to itself "dear, dear! I shall be too late!" (when she thought it over after- -wards, it occurred to her that she ought to have wondered at this, but at the time it all seemed quite natural); but when the rabbit actually took a watch out of its waistcoat-pocket, looked at it, and then hurried on, Alice started to her feet, for

it flashed across her mind that she had never
before seen a rabbit with either a waistcoat-pocket
or a watch to take out of it, and, full of curiosity,
she hurried across the field after it, and was just
in time to see it pop down a large rabbit-hole
under the hedge. In a moment down went Alice
after it, never once considering how in the world
she was to get out again.

The rabbit-hole went straight on like a
tunnel for some way, and then dipped suddenly
down, so suddenly, that Alice had not a moment
to think about stopping herself, before she found
herself falling down what seemed a deep well.
Either the well was very deep, or she fell very
slowly, for she had plenty of time as she went
down to look about her, and to wonder what
would happen next. First, she tried to look
down and make out what she was coming to,
but it was too dark to see anything: then, she
looked at the sides of the well, and noticed
that they were filled with cupboards and book-
-shelves; here and there were maps and pictures
hung on pegs. She took a jar down off one of
of the shelves as she passed: it was labelled

"Orange Marmalade", but to her great disappoint-
-ment it was empty: she did not like to drop
the jar, for fear of killing somebody underneath,
so managed to put it into one of the cupboards
as she fell past it.

"Well!" thought Alice to herself, "after such
a fall as this, I shall think nothing of tumbling
down stairs! How brave they'll all think me
at home! Why, I wouldn't say anything about
it, even if I fell off the top of the house!" (which
was most likely true.)

Down, down, down. Would the fall _never_
come to an end? "I wonder how many miles I've
fallen by this time?" said she aloud, "I must
be getting somewhere near the centre of the
earth. Let me see: that would be four thousand
miles down, I think —" (for you see Alice had
learnt several things of this sort in her lessons
in the schoolroom, and though this was not a
very good opportunity of showing off her know-
-ledge, as there was no one to hear her, still
it was good practice to say it over,) "yes, that's
the right distance, but then what Longitude
or Latitude-line shall I be in?" (Alice had no idea

what Longitude was, or Latitude either, but she thought they were nice grand words to say.)

Presently she began again: "I wonder if I shall fall right <u>through</u> the earth! How funny it'll be to come out among the people that walk with their heads downwards! But I shall have to ask them what the name of the country is, you know. Please, Ma'am, is this New Zealand or Australia?" – and she tried to curtsey as she spoke, (fancy <u>curtseying</u> as you're falling through the air! do you think you could manage it?) "and what an ignorant little girl she'll think me for asking! No, it'll never do to ask: perhaps I shall see it written up somewhere."

Down, down, down: there was nothing else to do, so Alice soon began talking again. "Dinah will miss me very much tonight, I should think!" (Dinah was the cat.) "I hope they'll remember her saucer of milk at tea-time! Oh, dear Dinah, I wish I had you here! There are no mice in the air, I'm afraid, but you might catch a bat, and that's very like a mouse, you know, my dear. But do cats eat bats, I wonder?" And here Alice began to get rather sleepy, and kept on saying to herself, in a dreamy sort of way "do cats eat bats? do cats eat bats?" and sometimes, "do bats eat cats?" for, as she couldn't answer either question, it didn't much matter which way she put it. She felt that she was dozing off, and had just begun to dream that she was walking hand in hand with Dinah, and was saying to her very earnestly, "Now, Dinah, my dear, tell me the truth. Did you ever eat a bat?" when suddenly, bump! bump! down she came upon a heap of sticks and shavings, and the fall was over.

Alice was not a bit hurt, and jumped on to her feet directly: she looked up, but it was all dark overhead; before her was another long passage, and the white rabbit was still in sight, hurrying down it. There was not a moment to be lost: away went Alice like the wind, and just heard it say, as it turned a corner, "my ears and whiskers, how late it's getting!" She turned the corner after it, and instantly found herself in a long, low hall, lit up by a row of lamps which hung from the roof.

There were doors all round the hall, but they were all locked, and when Alice had been all round it, and tried them all, she walked sadly down the middle, wondering

how she was ever to get out again: suddenly
she came upon a little three-legged table,
all made of solid glass; there was nothing
lying upon it, but a tiny golden key, and
Alice's first idea was that it might belong
to one of the doors of the hall, but alas! either
the locks were too large,
or the key too small, but
at any rate it would open
none of them. However, on
the second time round, she
came to a low curtain,
behind which was a door
about eighteen inches high:
she tried the little key in
the keyhole, and it fitted! Alice opened the door,
and looked down a small passage, not larger
than a rat-hole, into the loveliest garden you
ever saw. How she longed to get out of that
dark hall, and wander about among those beds
of bright flowers and those cool fountains, but
she could not even get her head through the
doorway, "and even if my head would go through,"
thought poor Alice, "it would be very little use
without my shoulders. Oh, how I wish I could shut

up like a telescope! I think I could, if I only knew how to begin." For, you see, so many out-of-the-way things had happened lately, that Alice began to think very few things indeed were really impossible.

There was nothing else to do, so she went back to the table, half hoping she might find another key on it, or at any rate a book of rules for shutting up people like telescopes : this time there was a little bottle on it — "which certainly was not there before" said Alice — and tied round the neck of the bottle was a paper label with the words DRINK ME beautifully printed on it in large letters.

It was all very well to say "drink me", "but I'll look first," said the wise little Alice, "and see whether the bottle's marked "poison" or not," for Alice had read several nice little stories about children that got burnt, and eaten up by wild beasts, and other unpleasant things, because they would not remember the simple rules their friends had given them, such as, that, if you get into the fire, it will burn you, and that, if you cut your finger very deeply with a knife, it generally bleeds, and she had never forgotten that, if you drink a bottle marked "poison", it is almost certain to disagree with you, sooner or later.

However, this bottle was <u>not</u> marked poison, so Alice tasted it, and finding it very nice, (it had, in fact, a sort of mixed flavour of cherry-tart, custard, pine-apple, roast turkey, toffy, and hot buttered toast,) she very soon finished it off.

*　　*　　*　　*　　*　　*

"What a curious feeling!" said Alice, "I must be shutting up like a telescope."

It was so indeed: she was now only ten inches high, and her face brightened up as it occurred to her that she was now the right size for going through the little door into that lovely garden. First, however, she waited for a few minutes to see whether she was going to shrink any further: she felt a little nervous about this, " for it "might end, you know," said Alice to herself, "in my going out altogether, like a candle, and what should I be like then, I wonder?" and she tried to fancy what the flame of a candle is like after the candle is blown out, for she could not remember having ever seen one. However, nothing more happened, so she decided on going into the garden at once, but, alas for poor Alice! when she got to the door, she found she had forgotten the little golden key, and when she went back to the table for the key, she found she could not possibly reach it: she could see it plainly enough through the glass, and she tried her best to climb up one of the legs of the table, but it was too slippery, and when she had tired herself out with trying, the poor little thing sat down and cried

"Come! there's no use in crying!" said Alice to herself rather sharply, "I advise you to leave off this minute!" (she generally gave herself very good advice, and sometimes scolded herself so severely as to bring tears into her eyes, and once she remembered boxing her own ears for having been unkind to herself in a game of croquet she was playing with herself, for this curious child was very fond of pretending to be two people,) "but it's no use now", thought poor Alice, "to pretend to be two people! Why, there's hardly enough of me left to make one respectable person!"

Soon her eyes fell on a little ebony box lying under the table : she opened it, and found in it a very small cake, on which was lying a card with the words EAT ME beautifully printed on it in large letters. "I'll eat," said Alice, "and if it makes me larger, I can reach the key, and if it makes me smaller, I can creep under the door, so either way I'll get into the garden, and I don't care which happens!"

She eat a little bit, and said anxiously to herself "which way? which way?" and laid her hand on the top of her head to feel which way it was growing, and was quite surprised to find that she remained the same size: to be sure this is what generally happens when one eats cake, but Alice had got into the way of expecting nothing but out-
-of-the way things to happen, and it seemed

quite dull and stupid for things to
go on in the common way.

So she set to work, and very
soon finished off the cake.

*   *   *   *   *

"Curiouser and curiouser!" cried
Alice, (she was so surprised that she
quite forgot how to speak good English,)
"now I'm opening out like the largest
telescope that ever was! Goodbye,
feet!" (for when she looked down
at her feet, they seemed almost
out of sight, they were getting so
far off,) "oh, my poor little feet, I
wonder who will put on your shoes
and stockings for you now, dears?
I'm sure I ca'nt! I shall be a great
deal too far off to bother myself about
you : you must manage the best
way you can — but I must be kind
to them", thought Alice, "or perhaps
they won't walk the way I want
to go! Let me see : I'll give them
a new pair of boots every Christmas".

And she went on planning
to herself how she would manage it:

"they must go by the carrier," she thought, "and how funny it'll seem, sending presents to one's own feet! And how odd the directions will look! ALICE'S RIGHT FOOT, ESQ.

THE CARPET,

with ALICE'S LOVE

oh dear! what nonsense I am talking!"

Just at this moment, her head struck against the roof of the hall: in fact, she was now rather more than nine feet high, and she at once took up the little golden key, and hurried off to the garden door.

Poor Alice! it was as much as she could do, lying down on one side, to look through into the garden with one eye, but to get through was more hopeless than ever: she sat down and cried again.

. "You ought to be ashamed of yourself," said Alice, "a great girl like you," (she might well say this,) "to cry in this way! Stop this instant, I tell you!" But she cried on all the same, shedding gallons of tears, until there was a large pool, about four inches deep, all round her, and reaching half way across the hall. After a time, she heard a little pattering of feet in the distance, and

dried her eyes to
see what was coming.
It was the white
rabbit coming back
again, splendidly
dressed, with a
pair of white kid
gloves in one hand,
and a nosegay in
the other. Alice was ready to ask help of any
one, she felt so desperate, and as the rabbit
passed her, she said, in a low, timid voice,
"If you please, Sir ⸺ " the rabbit started
violently, looked up once into the roof of
the hall, from which the voice seemed to come,
and then dropped the nosegay and the white
kid gloves, and skurried away into the dark-
-ness as hard as it could go.

Alice took up the nosegay and gloves,
and found the nosegay so delicious that
she kept smelling at it all the time she
went on talking to herself ⸺ "dear, dear!
how queer everything is today! and yester-
-day everything happened just as usual:
I wonder if I was changed in the night?
Let me think: was I the same when I
got up this morning? I think I remember

feeling rather different. But if I'm not the same, who in the world am I? Ah, that's the great puzzle!" And she began thinking over all the children she knew of the same age as herself, to see if she could have been changed for any of them.

"I'm sure I'm not Gertrude," she said, "for her hair goes in such long ringlets, and mine doesn't go in ringlets at all — and I'm sure I can't be Florence, for I know all sorts of things, and she, oh! she knows such a very little! Besides, <u>she's</u> she, and <u>I'm</u> I, and — oh dear! how puzzling it all is! I'll try if I know all the things I used to know. Let me see: four times five is twelve, and four times six is thirteen, and four times seven is fourteen — oh dear! I shall never get to twenty at this rate! But the Multiplication Table don't signify — let's try Geography. London is the capital of France, and Rome is the capital of Yorkshire, and Paris — oh dear! dear! that's all wrong, I'm certain! I must have been changed for Florence! I'll try and say "How doth the little"," and she crossed her hands on her

lap, and began, but her voice sounded
hoarse and strange, and the words did not
sound the same as they used to do:

"How doth the little crocodile
    Improve its shining tail,
And pour the waters of the Nile
    On every golden scale!

How cheerfully it seems to grin!
    How neatly spreads its claws!
And welcomes little fishes in
    With gently-smiling jaws!"

"I'm sure those are not the right
words", said poor Alice, and her eyes filled
with tears as she thought "I must be
Florence after all, and I shall have to go and
live in that poky little house, and have
next to no toys to play with, and oh! ever
so many lessons to learn! No! I've made
up my mind about it: if I'm Florence,
I'll stay down here! It'll be no use their
putting their heads down and saying 'come
up, dear!' I shall only look up and say

'who am I, then? answer me that first, and then, if I like being that person, I'll come up: if not, I'll stay down here till I'm somebody else — but, oh dear!" cried Alice with a sudden burst of tears, "I do wish they <u>would</u> put their heads down! I am so tired of being all alone here!"

As she said this, she looked down at her hands, and was surprised to find she had put on one of the rabbit's little gloves while she was talking. "How <u>can</u> I have done that?" thought she, "I must be growing small again". She got up and went to the table to measure herself by it, and found that, as nearly as she could guess, she was now about two feet high, and was going on shrinking rapidly: soon she found out that the reason of it was the nosegay she held in her hand: she dropped it hastily, just in time to save herself from shrinking away altogether, and found that she was now only three inches high.

"Now for the garden!" cried Alice,

as she hurried back to the little door;
but the little door was locked again, and
the little gold key was lying on the glass
table as before, and "things are worse
than ever!" thought the poor little girl,
"for I never was as small as this before,
never! And I declare it's too bad, it is!"

At this moment
her foot slipped,
and splash! she
was up to her chin
in salt water. Her
first idea was
that she had
fallen into the
sea: then she
remembered that
she was under
ground, and she
soon made out that it was the pool of tears she
had wept when she was nine feet high. "I wish
I hadn't cried so much!" said Alice, as she
swam about, trying to find her way out, "I
shall be punished for it now, I suppose, by
being drowned in my own tears! Well! that'll

be a queer thing, to be sure! However, every thing is queer today." Very soon she saw something splashing about in the pool near her: at first she thought it must be a walrus or a hippopotamus, but then she remembered how small she was herself, and soon made out that it was only a mouse, that had slipped in like herself.

"Would it be any use, now," thought Alice, "to speak to this mouse? The rabbit "is something quite out-of-the-way, no doubt, and so have I been, ever since I came down here, but that is no reason why the mouse should not be able to talk. I think I may as well try."

So she began: "oh Mouse, do you "know how to get out of this pool? I am very tired of swimming about here, oh Mouse!" The mouse looked at her rather inquisitively, and seemed to her to wink with one of its little eyes, but it said nothing.

"Perhaps it doesn't understand English," thought Alice; "I daresay it's a French mouse, come over with William the Conqueror!" (for,

with all her knowledge of history, Alice had no very clear notion how long ago anything had happened,) so she began again: "où est "ma chatte?" which was the first sentence out of her French lesson-book. The mouse gave a sudden jump in the pool, and seemed to quiver with fright: "oh, I beg your pardon!" cried Alice hastily, afraid that she had hurt the poor animal's feelings, "I quite forgot "you didn't like cats!"

"Not like cats!" cried the mouse, in a shrill, passionate voice, "would you like cats if you were me?"

"Well, perhaps not," said Alice in a soothing tone, "don't be angry about it. "And yet I wish I could show you our cat Dinah: I think you'd take a fancy to cats if you could only see her. She is such a dear quiet thing," said Alice, half to herself, as she swam lazily about in the pool, "she sits purring so nicely by the fire, licking her paws and washing her face: and she is such a nice soft thing to nurse, and she's such a capital one for catching mice — oh! I beg your pardon!" cried poor Alice

again, for this time the mouse was bristling
all over, and she felt certain that it was
really offended, "have I offended you?"

"Offended indeed!" cried the mouse, who
seemed to be positively trembling with rage,
"our family always _hated_ cats! Nasty, low,
vulgar things! Don't talk to me about them
any more!"

"I won't indeed!" said Alice, in a great
hurry to change the conversation, "are you—
"are you — fond of — dogs?" The mouse did
not answer, so Alice went on eagerly: "there
is such a nice little dog near our house
I should like to show you! A little bright—
—eyed terrier, you know, with oh! such long
curly brown hair! And it'll fetch things when
you throw them, and it'll sit up and beg
for its dinner, and all sorts of things — I
can't remember half of them — and it
belongs to a farmer, and he says it kills
all the rats and — oh dear!" said Alice
sadly, "I'm afraid I've offended it again!"
for the mouse was swimming away from
her as hard as it could go, and making
quite a commotion in the pool as it went.

So she called softly after it : "mouse dear! Do come back again, and we won't talk about cats and dogs any more, if you don't like them!" When the mouse heard this, it turned and swam slowly back to her : its face was quite pale, (with passion, Alice thought,) and it said in a trembling low voice "let's get to the shore, and then I'll tell you my history, and you'll understand why it is I hate cats and dogs".

It was high time to go, for the pool was getting quite full of birds and animals that had fallen into it. There was a Duck and a Dodo, a Lory and an Eaglet, and several other curious creatures. Alice led the way, and the whole party swam to the shore.

Chapter II

They were indeed
a curious looking
party that assembled
on the bank — the
birds with draggled
feathers, the animals
with their fur clinging
close to them — all
uncomfortable. The
dripping wet, cross, and first question of course was, how to get dry:
they had a consultation about this, and Alice
hardly felt at all surprised at finding her-
-self talking familiarly with the birds, as
if she had known them all her life. Indeed,
she had quite a long argument with the
Lory, who at last turned sulky, and would
only say "I am older than you, and must
know best", and this Alice would not admit
without knowing how old the Lory was, and
as the Lory positively refused to tell its
age, there was nothing more to be said.

At last the mouse, who seemed to have some authority among them, called out "sit down, all of you, and attend to me! I'll soon make you dry enough!" They all sat down at once, shivering, in a large ring, Alice in the middle, with her eyes anxiously fixed on the mouse, for she felt sure she would catch a bad cold if she did not get dry very soon.

"Ahem!" said the mouse, with a self-important air, "are you all ready? This is the driest thing I know. Silence all round, if you please!

"William the Conqueror, whose cause was favoured by the pope, was soon submitted to by the English, who wanted leaders, and had been of late much accustomed to usurpation and conquest. Edwin and Morcar, the earls of Mercia and Northumbria ——"

"Ugh!" said the Lory with a shiver.

"I beg your pardon?" said the mouse, frowning, but very politely, "did you speak?"

"Not I!" said the Lory hastily.

"I thought you did," said the mouse, "I proceed. Edwin and Morcar, the earls of Mercia and Northumbria, declared for him;

and even Stigand, the patriotic archbishop of Canterbury, found it advisable to go with Edgar Atheling to meet William and offer him the crown. William's conduct was at first moderate — how are you getting on now, dear?" said the mouse, turning to Alice as it spoke.

"As wet as ever," said poor Alice," it doesn't seem to dry me at all".

"In that case," said the Dodo solemnly, rising to his feet," I move that the meeting adjourn, for the immediate adoption of more energetic remedies — "

"Speak English!" said the Duck," I don't know the meaning of half those long words, and what's more, I don't believe you do either!" And the Duck quacked a comfortable laugh to itself. Some of the other birds tittered audibly.

"I only meant to say," said the Dodo in a rather offended tone," that I know of a house near here, where we could get the young lady and the rest of the party dried, and then we could listen comfortably to the story which I think you were good enough to promise to tell us," bowing gravely to the mouse.

The mouse made no objection to this,
and the whole party moved along the river
bank, (for the pool had by this time began
to flow out of the hall, and the edge of it
was fringed with rushes and forget-me-nots,)
in a slow procession, the Dodo leading the
way. After a time the Dodo became impatient,
and, leaving the Duck to bring up the rest
of the party, moved on at a quicker pace
with Alice, the Lory, and the Eaglet, and
soon brought them to a little cottage, and
there they sat snugly by the fire, wrapped
up in blankets, until the rest of the party
had arrived, and they were all dry again.

Then they all sat down again in a
large ring on the bank, and begged the
mouse to begin his story.

"Mine is a long and a sad tale!" said
the mouse, turning to Alice, and sighing.

"It _is_ a long tail, certainly," said
Alice, looking down with wonder at the
mouse's tail, which was coiled nearly all
round the party, "but why do you call it sad?"
and she went on puzzling about this as
the mouse went on speaking, so that her
idea of the tale was something like this:

We lived beneath the mat
Warm and snug and fat
But one woe, & that
Was the cat!
To our joys
a clog, In
our eyes a
fog, On our
hearts a log
Was the dog!
When the
cat's away,
Then
the mice
will
play,
But, alas!
one day, (So they say)
Came the dog and
cat, Hunting
for a
rat,
Crushed
the mice
all flat,
Each
one
as
he
sat
Underneath the mat, Warm & snug, & fat. — Think of that!

"You are not attending!" said the mouse to Alice severely, "what are you thinking of?"

"I beg your pardon," said Alice very humbly, "you had got to the fifth bend, I think?"

"I had <u>not</u>!" cried the mouse, sharply and very angrily.

"A knot!" said Alice, always ready to make herself useful, and looking anxiously about her, "oh, do let me help to undo it!"

"I shall do nothing of the sort!" said the mouse, getting up and walking away from the party, "you insult me by talking such nonsense!"

"I didn't mean it!" pleaded poor Alice, "but you're so easily offended, you know."

The mouse only growled in reply.

"Please come back and finish your story!" Alice called after it, and the others all joined in chorus "yes, please do!" but the mouse only shook its ears, and walked quickly away, and was soon out of sight.

"What a pity it wouldn't stay!" sighed the Lory, and an old Crab took the oppor-tunity of saying to its daughter "Ah, my dear!

let this be a lesson to you never to lose your temper!" "Hold your tongue, Ma!" said the young Crab, a little snappishly, "you're enough to try the patience of an oyster!"

"I wish I had our Dinah here, I know I do!" said Alice aloud, addressing no one in particular, "she'd soon fetch it back!"

"And who is Dinah, if I might venture to ask the question?" said the Lory.

Alice replied eagerly, for she was always ready to talk about her pet, "Dinah's our cat. And she's such a capital one for catching mice, you can't think! And oh! I wish you could see her after the birds! Why, she'll eat a little bird as soon as look at it!"

This answer caused a remarkable sensation among the party; some of the birds hurried off at once; one old magpie began wrapping itself up very carefully, remarking "I really must be getting home: the night air does not suit my throat," and a canary called out in a trembling voice to its children "come away from her, my dears, she's no fit company for you!" On various pretexts, they all moved off, and Alice was soon left alone.

She sat for some while sorrowful and silent, but she was not long before she recovered her spirits, and began talking to herself again as usual: "I do wish some of them had stayed a little longer! and I was getting to be such friends with them — really the Lory and I were almost like sisters! and so was that dear little Eaglet! And then the Duck and the Dodo! How nicely the Duck sang to us as we came along through the water: and if the Dodo hadn't known the way to that nice little cottage, I don't know when we should have got dry again ——" and there is no knowing how long she might have prattled on in this way, if she had not suddenly caught the sound of pattering feet.

It was the white rabbit, trotting slowly back again, and looking anxiously about it as it went, as if it had lost something, and she heard it muttering to itself "the Marchioness! the Marchioness! oh my dear paws! oh my fur and whiskers! She'll have me executed, as sure as ferrets

are ferrets! Where _can_ I have dropped them,
I wonder?" Alice guessed in a moment that
it was looking for the nosegay and the pair
of white kid gloves, and she began hunting
for them, but they were now nowhere to be
seen — everything seemed to have changed
since her swim in the pool, and her walk
along the river-bank with its fringe of
rushes and forget-me-nots, and the glass
table and the little door had vanished.

Soon the rabbit
noticed Alice, as
she stood looking
curiously about
her, and at once
said in a quick
angry tone, "why,
Mary Ann! what
are you doing out
here? Go home this
moment, and look
on my dressing-table for my gloves and nosegay,
and fetch them here, as quick as you can
run, do you hear?" and Alice was so much
frightened that she ran off at once, without

saying a word, in the direction which the rabbit had pointed out

She soon found herself in front of a neat little house, on the door of which was a bright brass plate with the name **W. RABBIT, ESQ.** she went in, and hurried upstairs, for fear she should meet the real Mary Ann and be turned out of the house before she had found the gloves: she knew that one pair had been lost in the hall, "but of course", thought Alice, "it has plenty more of them in its house. How queer it seems to be going messages for a rabbit! I suppose Dinah'll be sending me messages next!" And she began fancying the sort of things that would happen: "Miss Alice! come here directly and get ready for your walk!" "Coming in a minute, nurse! but I've got to watch this mousehole till Dinah comes back, and see that the mouse doesnt get out ____" "only I don't think," Alice went on, "that they'd let Dinah stop in the house, if it began ordering people about like that!"

By this time she had found her
way into a tidy little room, with a
table in the window on which was a
looking-glass and, (as Alice had hoped,)
two or three pairs of tiny white kid gloves:
she took up a pair of gloves, and was just
going to leave the room, when her eye fell
upon a little bottle that stood near the
looking-glass: there was no label on it
this time with the words "drink me", but
nevertheless she uncorked it and put it

to her lips: "I
know something
interesting is
sure to happen,"
she said to herself,
"whenever I eat
or drink anything,
so I'll see what
this bottle does.
I do hope it'll
make me grow
larger, for I'm quite tired of being such a
tiny little thing!"

It did so indeed, and much sooner

than she expected: before she had drunk half the bottle, she found her head pressing against the ceiling, and she stooped to save her neck from being broken, and hastily put down the bottle, saying to herself "that's

quite enough— I hope I sha'n't grow any more— I wish I hadn't drunk so much!"

Alas! it was too late: she went on growing and growing, and very soon had to kneel down: in another minute there was not room even for this, and she tried the effect of lying down, with one elbow against the door, and the other arm curled round her head. Still she went on growing, and as a last resource she put one arm out of the window, and one foot up the chimney, and said to herself "now I can do no more — what will become of me?"

Luckily for Alice, the little magic bottle had now had its full effect, and she grew no larger: still it was very uncomfortable, and as there seemed to be no sort of chance of ever getting out of the room again, no wonder she felt unhappy. "It was much pleasanter at home," thought poor Alice, "when one wasn't always growing larger and smaller, and being ordered about by mice and rabbits — I almost wish I hadn't gone down that rabbit-hole, and yet, and yet — it's rather curious, you know, this sort of life. I do wonder what can have happened to me! When I used to read fairy-tales, I fancied that sort of thing never happened, and now here I am in the middle of one! There ought to be a book written about me, that there ought! and when I grow up I'll write one — but I'm grown up now" said she in a sorrowful tone, "at least there's no room to grow up any more here."

"But then", thought Alice, "shall I never get any older than I am now? That'll be a comfort, one way — never to be an old woman — but then — always to have lessons to learn! Oh, I shouldn't like <u>that</u>!"

"Oh, you foolish Alice!" she said again, "how can you learn lessons in here? Why, there's hardly room for you, and no room at all for any lesson-books!"

And so she went on, taking first one side, and then the other, and making quite a conversation of it altogether, but after a few minutes she heard a voice outside, which made her stop to listen.

"Mary Ann! Mary Ann!" said the voice, "fetch me my gloves this moment!" Then came a little pattering of feet on the stairs: Alice knew it was the rabbit coming to look for her, and she trembled till she shook the house, quite forgetting that she was now about a thousand times as large as the rabbit, and had no reason to be afraid of it. Presently the rabbit came to the door, and tried to open it, but as it opened inwards, and Alice's elbow was against it, the attempt proved a failure. Alice heard it say to itself "then I'll go round and get in at the window."

"<u>That</u> you won't!" thought Alice, and, after waiting till she fancied she heard the rabbit just under the window, she

suddenly spread out her hand, and made a snatch in the air. She did not get hold of anything, but she heard a little shriek and a fall and a crash of breaking glass, from which she concluded that it was just possible it had fallen into a cucumber-frame, or something of the sort.

Next came an angry voice — the rabbit's — "Pat, Pat! where are you?" And then a voice she had never heard before, "shure then I'm here! digging for apples, anyway, yer honour!"

"Digging for apples indeed!" said the rabbit angrily, "here, come and help me out of _this_!" — Sound of more breaking glass.

"Now, tell me, Pat, what is that coming out of the window?"

"Shure it's an arm, yer honour!" (He pronounced it "arrum".)

"An arm, you goose! Who ever saw an arm that size? Why, it fills the whole window, don't you see?"

"Shure, it does, yer honour, but it's an arm for all that."

"Well, it's no business there: go and take it away!"

There was a long silence after this, and Alice could only hear whispers now and then, such as "shure I don't like it, yer honour, at all at all!" "do as I tell you, you coward!" and at last she spread out her hand again and made another snatch in the air. This time there were _two_ little shrieks, and more breaking glass — "what a number of cucumber-frames there must be!" thought Alice, "I wonder what they'll do next! As for pulling me out of the window, I only wish they _could_! _I'm_ sure I don't want to stop in here any longer!"

She waited for some time without

hearing anything more: at last came a
rumbling of little cart-wheels, and the
sound of a good many voices all talking
together: she made out the words "where's
the other ladder? — why, I hadn't to bring
but one, Bill's got the other — here, put 'em
up at this corner — no, tie 'em together
first — they don't reach high enough yet —
oh, they'll do well enough, don't be particular —
here, Bill! catch hold of this rope — will
the roof bear? — mind that loose slate —
oh, it's coming down! heads below!" (a
loud crash) "now, who did that? — it was
Bill, I fancy — who's to go down the chimney?
— nay, I shan't! you do it! — that I
won't then — Bill's got to go down — here,
Bill! the master says you've to go down
the chimney!"

"Oh, so Bill's got to come down
the chimney, has he?" said Alice to herself,
"why, they seem to put everything upon
Bill! I wouldn't be in Bill's place for a
good deal: the fireplace is a pretty tight
one, but I think I can kick a little!"

She drew her foot as far down the
chimney as she could, and waited till she

heard a little
animal (she
couldn't guess
what sort it
was) scratching
and scrambling
in the chimney
close above her:
then, saying to
herself "this is
Bill", she gave
one sharp kick, and waited again to see what
would happen next.

The first thing was a general chorus
of "there goes Bill!" then the rabbit's voice
alone "catch him, you by the hedge!" then
silence, and then another confusion of voices,
"how was it, old fellow? what happened to
you? tell us all about it."

Last came a little feeble squeaking
voice, ("that's Bill" thought Alice,) which said
"well, I hardly know — I'm all of a fluster
myself — something comes at me like a
Jack-in-the-box, and the next minute up I
goes like a rocket!" "And so you did, old
fellow!" said the other voices.

"We must burn the house down!" said the voice of the rabbit, and Alice called out as loud as she could "if you do, I'll set Dinah at you!" This caused silence again, and while Alice was thinking "but how can I get Dinah here?" she found to her great delight that she was getting smaller: very soon she was able to get up out of the uncomfortable position in which she had been lying, and in two or three minutes more she was once more three inches high.

She ran out of the house as quick as she could, and found quite a crowd of little animals waiting outside — guinea-pigs, white mice, squirrels, and "Bill" a little green lizard, that was being supported in the arms of one of the guinea-pigs, while another was giving it something out of a bottle. They all made a rush at her the moment she appeared, but Alice ran her hardest, and soon found herself in a thick wood.

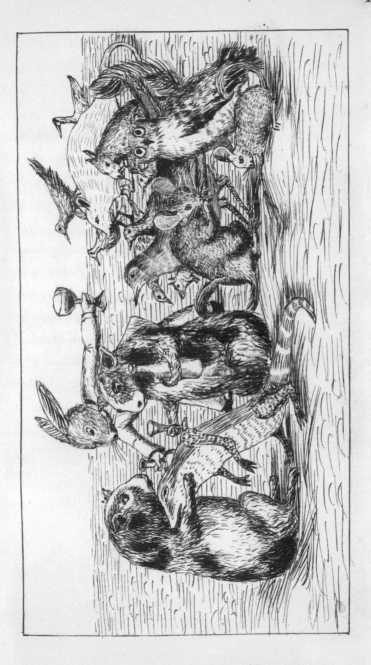

Chapter III

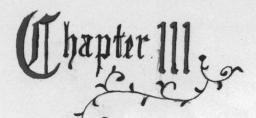

"The first thing I've got to do," said Alice to herself, as she wandered about in the wood, "is to grow to my right size, and the second thing is to find my way into that lovely garden. I think that will be the best plan".

It sounded an excellent plan, no doubt, and very neatly and simply arranged: the only difficulty was, that she had not the smallest idea how to set about it, and while she was peering anxiously among the trees round her, a little sharp bark just over her head made her look up in a great hurry.

An enormous puppy was looking down at her with large round eyes, and feebly stretching out one paw, trying to reach her: "poor thing!" said Alice in a coaxing tone, and she tried hard to whistle to it, but she was terribly alarmed all the while at the thought that it might be hungry, in which case it would probably devour her in spite of all her coaxing. Hardly knowing what she did, she picked up a little bit of stick, and held it out to the puppy: whereupon the puppy jumped into the air off all its feet at once, and with a yelp of delight rushed at the stick, and made believe to worry it: then Alice dodged behind a great thistle to keep herself from being run over, and, the moment she appeared at the other side, the puppy made another dart at the stick, and tumbled head over heels in its hurry to get hold: then Alice, thinking it was very like having a game of play with a cart-horse, and expecting every moment to be trampled under its feet, ran round the thistle again: then the puppy began a series of short charges at the stick, running a very little way forwards each time and a long way back, and barking hoarsely all the while, till at last it sat down a good way off, panting, with its tongue hanging out of its mouth, and its great eyes half shut.

This seemed to Alice a good opportunity for making her escape : she set off at once, and ran till the puppy's bark sounded quite faint in the distance, and till she was quite tired and out of breath.

"And yet what a dear little puppy it was!" said Alice, as she leant against a buttercup to rest herself, and fanned herself with her hat, "I should have liked teaching it tricks, if —— if I'd only been the right size to do it! Oh! I'd nearly forgotten that I've got to grow up again! Let me see : how is it to be managed? I suppose I ought to eat or drink something or other, but the great question is, what?"

The great question certainly was, what? Alice looked all round her at the flowers and the blades of grass, but could not see anything that looked like the right thing to eat under the circumstances. There was a large mushroom near her, about the same height as herself, and when she had looked under it, and on both sides of it, and behind it, it occurred to her to look and see what was on the top of it.

She stretched herself up on tiptoe, and peeped over the edge of the mushroom,

and her eyes immediately met those of a large blue caterpillar, which was sitting with its arms folded, quietly smoking a long hookah, and taking not the least notice of her or of anything else.

For some time they looked at each other in silence: at last the caterpillar took the hookah out of its mouth, and languidly addressed her.

"Who are you?" said the caterpillar.

This was not an encouraging opening for a conversation: Alice replied rather shyly, "I— I hardly know, sir, just at present— at least I know who I _was_ when I got up this morning, but I think I must have been changed several times since that."

"What do you mean by that?" said the caterpillar, "explain yourself!"

"I ca'nt explain _myself_, I'm afraid, sir,"

said Alice, "because I'm not myself, you see".

"I don't see", said the caterpillar.

"I'm afraid I can't put it more clearly," Alice replied very politely, "for I can't under-stand it myself, and really to be so many different sizes in one day is very confusing."

"It isn't," said the caterpillar.

"Well, perhaps you haven't found it so yet," said Alice, "but when you have to turn into a chrysalis, you know, and then after that into a butterfly, I should think it'll feel a little queer, don't you think so?"

"Not a bit," said the caterpillar.

"All I know is," said Alice, "it would feel queer to _me_."

"_You_!" said the caterpillar contemptu-ously, "who are you?"

Which brought them back again to the beginning of the conversation: Alice felt a little irritated at the caterpillar making such very short remarks, and she drew her-self up and said very gravely "I think you ought to tell me who _you_ are, first."

"Why?" said the caterpillar.

Here was another puzzling question:

and as Alice had no reason ready, and the caterpillar seemed to be in a very bad temper, she turned round and walked away.

"Come back!" the caterpillar called after her, "I've something important to say!"

This sounded promising: Alice turned and came back again.

"Keep your temper," said the caterpillar.

"Is that all?" said Alice, swallowing down her anger as well as she could.

"No," said the caterpillar.

Alice thought she might as well wait, as she had nothing else to do, and perhaps after all the caterpillar might tell her something worth hearing. For some minutes it puffed away at its hookah without speaking, but at last it unfolded its arms, took the hookah out of its mouth again, and said "so you think you're changed, do you?"

"Yes, sir," said Alice, "I can't remember the things I used to know — I've tried to say "How doth the little busy bee" and it came all different!"

"Try and repeat "You are old, father William"," said the caterpillar.

Alice folded her hands, and began:

1.

"You are old, father William," the young man said,
  "And your hair is exceedingly white:
And yet you incessantly stand on your head —
  Do you think, at your age, it is right?"

2.

"In my youth," father William replied to his son,
  "I feared it might injure the brain:
But now that I'm perfectly sure I have none,
  Why, I do it again and again."

3.

"You are old," said the youth, "as I mentioned before,
    "And have grown most uncommonly fat:
Yet you turned a back-somersault in at the door —
    Pray what is the reason of that ?"

4.

"In my youth," said the sage, as he shook his gray locks,
    "I kept all my limbs very supple.
By the use of this ointment, five shillings the box —
    Allow me to sell you a couple."

5.

"You are old," said the youth, "and your jaws are too weak
"For anything tougher than suet :
Yet you eat all the goose, with the bones and the beak —
Pray, how did you manage to do it ?"

5.

"In my youth," said the old man, "I took to the law,
And argued each case with my wife,
And the muscular strength, which it gave to my jaw,
Has lasted the rest of my life."

7.

"You are old", said the youth, "one would hardly suppose

"That your eye was as steady as ever:

Yet you balanced an eel on the end of your nose ——

What made you so awfully clever ? "

8.

"I have answered three questions, and that is enough,"

Said his father, "don't give yourself airs !

"Do you think I can listen all day to such stuff ?

Be off, or I'll kick you down stairs ! "

"That is not said right," said the caterpillar.

"Not quite right, I'm afraid," said Alice timidly, "some of the words have got altered."

"It is wrong from beginning to end," said the caterpillar decidedly, and there was silence for some minutes: the caterpillar was the first to speak.

"What size do you want to be?" it asked.

"Oh, I'm not particular as to size," Alice hastily replied, "only one doesn't like changing so often, you know."

"Are you content now?" said the caterpillar.

"Well, I should like to be a little larger, sir, if you wouldn't mind," said Alice, "three inches is such a wretched height to be."

"It is a very good height indeed!" said the caterpillar loudly and angrily, rearing itself straight up as it spoke (it was exactly three inches high).

"But I'm not used to it!" pleaded poor Alice in a piteous tone, and she thought to herself "I wish the creatures wouldn't be so easily offended!"

"You'll get used to it in time", said the caterpillar, and it put the hookah into its mouth, and began smoking again.

This time Alice waited quietly until it chose to speak again: in a few minutes the caterpillar took the hookah out of its mouth, and got down off the mushroom, and crawled away into the grass, merely remarking as it went: "the top will make you grow taller, and the stalk will make you grow shorter."

"The top of _what_? the stalk of _what_?" thought Alice.

"Of the mushroom," said the caterpillar, just as if she had asked it aloud, and in another moment it was out of sight.

Alice remained looking thoughtfully at the mushroom for a minute, and then picked it and carefully broke it in two,

taking the stalk in one hand, and the top in the other. "Which does the stalk do?" she said, and nibbled a little bit of it to try: the next mo--ment she felt a violent blow on her chin: it had struck her foot!

She was a good deal frightened by this very sudden change, but as she did not shrink any further, and had not dropped the top of the mushroom, she did not give up hope yet. There was hardly room to open her mouth, with her chin pressing against her foot, but she did it at last, and managed to bite off a little bit of the top of the mushroom.

 *   *   *   *   *

"Come! my head's free at last!" said Alice in a tone of delight, which changed into alarm in another mo- -ment, when she found that her shoulders were nowhere to be seen: she looked down upon an immense length of neck, which seemed to rise like a stalk out of a sea of green leaves that lay far below her.

"What can all that green stuff be?" said Alice, "and where have my shoulders got to? And oh! my poor hands! how is it I can't see you?" She was moving them about as she spoke, but no result seemed to follow, except a little rustling among the leaves. Then she tried to bring her head down to her hands, and was delighted to find that her neck would bend about easily in every direction, like a serpent. She had just succeeded in bending it down in a beautiful zig-zag, and was going to dive in among the leaves, which she found to be the tops of the trees of the wood she had been wandering in, when a sharp hiss made her draw back: a large pigeon had flown into her face, and was vio-lently beating her with its wings.

"Serpent!" screamed the pigeon. "I'm not a serpent!" said Alice indignantly, "let me alone!"

"I've tried every way!" the pigeon said desperately, with a kind of sob: "nothing seems to suit 'em!"

"I haven't the least idea what you mean," said Alice.

"I've tried the roots of trees, and I've tried banks, and I've tried hedges," the pigeon went on without attending to her, "but them serpents! There's no pleasing 'em!"

Alice was more and more puzzled, but she thought there was no use in saying anything till the pigeon had finished.

"As if it wasn't trouble enough hatching the eggs!" said the pigeon, "without being on the look out for serpents, day and night! Why, I haven't had a wink of sleep these three weeks!"

"I'm very sorry you've been annoyed," said Alice, beginning to see its meaning.

"And just as I'd taken the highest tree in the wood," said the pigeon raising its voice to a shriek, "and was just thinking I was free of 'em at last, they must needs come down from the sky! Ugh! Serpent!"

"But I'm _not_ a serpent," said Alice, "I'm a — I'm a —"

"Well! _What_ are you?" said the pigeon, "I see you're trying to invent something."

"I — I'm a little girl," said Alice, rather doubtfully, as she remembered the number of changes she had gone through.

"A likely story indeed!" said the pigeon, "I've seen a good many of them in my time, but never _one_ with such a neck as yours! No, you're a serpent, I know _that_ well enough! I suppose you'll tell me next that you never tasted an egg!"

"I _have_ tasted eggs, certainly," said Alice, who was a very truthful child, "but indeed I don't want any of yours. I don't like them raw."

"Well, be off, then!" said the pigeon, and settled down into its nest again. Alice crouched down among the trees, as well as she could, as her neck kept getting entangled among the branches, and several times she had to stop and untwist it. Soon she remembered the pieces of mushroom which she still held in her hands, and set to work very carefully, nibbling first at one and then at the other, and growing sometimes taller and sometimes shorter, until she had succeeded in bringing herself down to her usual size.

It was so long since she had been of the right size that it felt quite strange at first, but she got quite used to it in a minute or two, and began talking to herself as usual : "well! there's half my plan done now! How puzzling all these changes are! I'm never sure what I'm going to be, from one minute to another! However, I've got to my right size again : the next thing is, to get into that beautiful garden — how is that to be done, I wonder?"

Just as she said this, she noticed that one of the trees had a doorway leading right into it. "That's very curious!" she thought, "but everything's curious today : I may as well go in." And in she went.

Once more she found herself in the long hall, and close to the little glass table : "now, I'll manage better this time" she said to herself, and began by taking the little golden key, and unlocking the door that led into the garden. Then she set to work eating the pieces of mushroom till she was about fifteen inches high : then she walked down the little passage : and then — she found herself at last in the beautiful garden, among the bright flowerbeds and the cool fountains.

Chapter IV

A large rose tree stood near the entrance of the garden: the roses on it were white, but there were three gardeners at it, busily painting them red. This Alice thought a very curious thing, and she went near to watch them, and just as she came up she heard one of them say "look out, Five! Don't go splashing paint over me like that!"

"I couldn't help it", said Five in a sulky tone, "Seven jogged my elbow."

On which Seven lifted up his head and said "that's right, Five! Always lay the blame on others!"

"You'd better not talk!" said Five, "I

heard the Queen say only yesterday she thought of having you beheaded!"

"What for?" said the one who had spoken first.

"That's not your business, Two!" said Seven.

"Yes, it is his business!" said Five, "and I'll tell him: it was for bringing tulip-roots to the cook instead of potatoes."

Seven flung down his brush, and had just begun "well! Of all the unjust things—" when his eye fell upon Alice, and he stopped suddenly: the others looked round, and all of them took off their hats and bowed low.

"Would you tell me, please," said Alice timidly, "why you are painting those roses?"

Five and Seven looked at Two, but said nothing: Two began, in a low voice, "why, Miss, the fact is, this ought to have been a red rose tree, and we put a white one in by mistake, and if the Queen was to find it out, we should all have our heads cut off. So, you see, we're doing our best, before she comes, to—" At this moment Five, who had been looking anxiously across the garden called out "the Queen! the Queen!" and the three gardeners instantly threw them--selves flat upon their faces. There was a sound of many footsteps, and Alice looked round, eager to see the Queen.

First came ten soldiers carrying clubs: these were all shaped like the three gardeners, flat and oblong, with their hands and feet at the corners: next the ten courtiers; these were all ornamented with diamonds, and walked two and two, as the soldiers did. After these came the Royal children: there were ten of them, and the little dears came jumping merrily along, hand in hand, in couples: they were all ornamented with hearts. Next came the guests, mostly kings and queens, among whom Alice recognised the white rabbit: it was talking in a hurried nervous manner, smiling at everything that was said, and went by without noticing her. Then followed the Knave of Hearts, carrying the King's crown on a cushion, and, last of all this grand pro--cession, came THE KING AND QUEEN OF HEARTS.

When the procession came opposite to Alice, they all stopped and looked at her, and

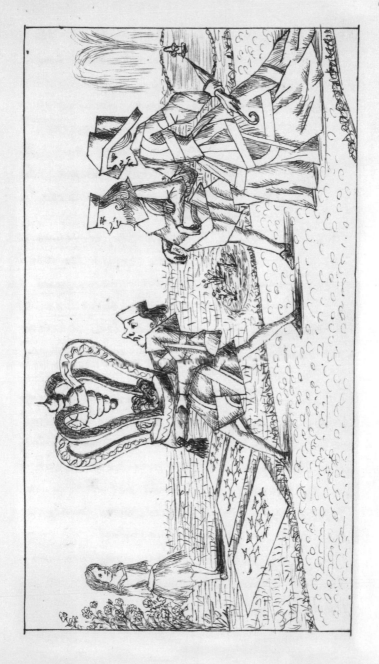

the Queen said severely "who is this?" She said
it to the Knave of Hearts, who only bowed and
smiled in reply.

"Idiot!" said the Queen, turning up her
nose, and asked Alice "what's your name?"

"My name is Alice, so please your Ma-
-jesty," said Alice boldly, for she thought to
herself "why, they're only a pack of cards! I
needn't be afraid of them!"

"Who are these?" said the Queen, pointing
to the three gardeners lying round the rose tree,
for, as they were lying on their faces, and the
pattern on their backs was the same as the
rest of the pack, she could not tell whether
they were gardeners, or soldiers, or courtiers, or
three of her own children.

"How should I know?" said Alice, surprised
at her own courage, "it's no business of mine."

The Queen turned crimson with fury,
and, after glaring at her for a minute, began in
a voice of thunder "off with her——"

"Nonsense!" said Alice, very loudly and
decidedly, and the Queen was silent.

The King laid his hand upon her arm, and
said timidly "remember, my dear! She is only
a child!"

The Queen turned angrily away from him, and said to the Knave "turn them over!"

The Knave did so, very carefully, with one foot.

"Get up!" said the Queen, in a shrill loud voice, and the three gardeners instantly jumped up, and began bowing to the King, the Queen, the Royal children, and everybody else.

"Leave off that!" screamed the Queen, "you make me giddy". And then, turning to the rose tree, she went on "what have you been doing here?"

"May it please your Majesty", said Two very humbly, going down on one knee as he spoke, "we were trying——"

"I see!" said the Queen, who had meanwhile been examining the roses, "off with their heads!" and the procession moved on, three of the soldiers remaining behind to execute the three unfortunate gardeners, who ran to Alice for protection.

"You shan't be beheaded!" said Alice, and she put them into her pocket: the three soldiers marched once round her, looking for them, and then quietly marched off after the others.

"Are their heads off?" shouted the Queen.

"Their heads are gone," the soldiers shouted in reply, "if it please your Majesty!"

"That's right!" shouted the Queen, "can you play croquet?"

The soldiers were silent, and looked at Alice, as the question was evidently meant for her.

"Yes!" shouted Alice at the top of her voice.

"Come on then!" roared the Queen, and Alice joined the procession, wondering very much what would happen next.

"It's— its a very fine day!" said a timid little voice : she was walking by the white rabbit, who was peeping anxiously into her face.

"Very," said Alice, "where's the Marchioness?"

"Hush, hush!" said the rabbit in a low voice, "she'll hear you. The Queen's the Marchioness : didn't you know that?"

"No, I didn't," said Alice, "what of?"

"Queen of Hearts," said the rabbit in a whisper, putting its mouth close to her ear, "and Marchioness of Mock Turtles."

"What are _they_?" said Alice, but there was no time for the answer, for they had reached the croquet-ground, and the game began instantly.

Alice thought she had never seen such a curious croquet-ground in all her life : it was all in ridges and furrows : the croquet-balls were live hedgehogs, the mallets live ostriches, and the soldiers had to double themselves up, and stand

on their feet and hands, to make the arches.

The chief difficulty which Alice found at first was to manage her ostrich: she got its body tucked away, comfortably enough, under

her arm, with its legs hanging down, but generally, just as she had got its neck straightened out nicely, and was going to give a blow with its head, it _would_ twist itself round, and look up into her face, with such a puzzled expression that she could not help bursting out laughing: and when she had got its head down, and was going to begin again, it was very confusing to find that the hedgehog had unrolled itself, and was in the act of crawling away: besides all this, there was generally a ridge or a furrow in her way, wherever she wanted to send the hedgehog to, and as the doubled-up soldiers were always getting up and walking off to other parts of the ground, Alice soon came to the conclusion that it was a very difficult game indeed.

The players all played at once without waiting for turns, and quarrelled all the while at the tops of their voices, and in a very few minutes the Queen was in a furious passion, and went stamping about and shouting "off with his head!" or "off with her head!" about once in a minute. All those whom she sentenced were taken into custody by the soldiers, who of course had to leave off being arches to do this, so that, by the end of half an hour or so, there were no arches left, and all the players, except the King, the Queen, and Alice, were in custody, and under sentence of execution.

Then the Queen left off, quite out of breath, and said to Alice "have you seen the Mock Turtle?"

"No," said Alice, "I don't even know what a Mock Turtle is."

"Come on then," said the Queen, "and it shall tell you its history."

As they walked off together, Alice heard the King say in a low voice, to the company generally, "you are all pardoned."

"Come, that's a good thing!" thought Alice, who had felt quite grieved at the number of executions which the Queen had ordered.

They very soon came upon a Gryphon, which lay fast asleep in the sun: (if you don't know what a Gryphon is, look at the picture): "up, lazy thing!" said the Queen, "and take this young lady to see the Mock Turtle, and to

hear its history. I must go back and see after some executions I ordered," and she walked off, leaving Alice with the Gryphon. Alice did not quite like the look of the creature, but on the whole she thought it quite as safe to stay as to go after that savage Queen: so she waited.

The Gryphon sat up and rubbed its eyes: then it watched the Queen till she was out of sight: then it chuckled. "What fun!" said the Gryphon, half to itself, half to Alice.

"What _is_ the fun?" said Alice.

"Why, _she_," said the Gryphon; "it's all her fancy, that: they never executes nobody, you know: come on!"

"Everybody says 'come on!' here," thought Alice, as she walked slowly after the Gryphon; "I never was ordered about so before in all my life — never!"

They had not gone far before they saw the Mock Turtle in the distance, sitting sad and lonely on a little ledge of rock, and, as they

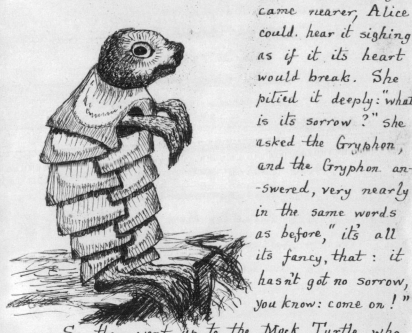

came nearer, Alice could hear it sighing as if it its heart would break. She pitied it deeply: "what is its sorrow?" she asked the Gryphon, and the Gryphon an--swered, very nearly in the same words as before," it's all its fancy, that: it hasn't got no sorrow, you know: come on!"

So they went up to the Mock Turtle, who looked at them with large eyes full of tears, but said nothing.

"This here young lady" said the Gryphon,

"wants for to know your history, she do."

"I'll tell it," said the Mock Turtle, in a deep hollow tone, "sit down, and don't speak till I've finished."

So they sat down, and no one spoke for some minutes: Alice thought to herself "I don't see how it can *ever* finish, if it doesn't begin," but she waited patiently.

"Once," said the Mock Turtle at last, with a deep sigh, "I was a real Turtle."

These words were followed by a very long silence, broken only by an occasional exclamation of "hjckrrh!" from the Gryphon, and the constant heavy sobbing of the Mock Turtle. Alice was very nearly getting up and saying, "thank you, sir, for your interesting story," but she could not help thinking there *must* be more to come, so she sat still and said nothing.

"When we were little," the Mock Turtle went on, more calmly, though still sobbing a little now and then, "we went to school in the sea. The master was an old Turtle — we used to call him Tortoise — "

"Why did you call him Tortoise, if he wasn't one?" asked Alice.

"We called him Tortoise because he taught us," said the Mock Turtle angrily, "really you are very dull!"

"You ought to be ashamed of yourself for asking such a simple question," added the Gryphon, and then they both sat silent and looked at poor Alice, who felt ready to sink into the earth: at last the Gryphon said to the Mock Turtle, "get on, old fellow! Don't be all day!" and the Mock Turtle went on in these words:

"You may not have lived much under the sea—" ("I haven't," said Alice,) "and perhaps you were never even introduced to a lobster——" (Alice began to say "I once tasted—" but hastily checked herself, and said "no, never," instead,) "so you can have no idea what a delightful thing a Lobster Quadrille is!"

"No, indeed," said Alice, "what sort of a thing is it?"

"Why," said the Gryphon, "you form into a line along the sea shore—"

"Two lines!" cried the Mock Turtle, "seals, turtles, salmon, and so on—advance twice—"

"Each with a lobster as partner!" cried the Gryphon.

."Of course", the Mock Turtle said, "advance twice, set to partners ——— "

"Change lobsters, and retire in same order ——" interrupted the Gryphon.

"Then, you know," continued the Mock Turtle, "you throw the ——— "

"The lobsters!" shouted the Gryphon, with a bound into the air.

"As far out to sea as you can ——— "

"Swim after them!" screamed the Gryphon.

"Turn a somersault in the sea!" cried the Mock Turtle, capering wildly about.

"Change lobsters again!" yelled the Gryphon at the top of its voice, "and then ——— "

"That's all," said the Mock Turtle, suddenly dropping its voice, and the two creatures, who had been jumping about like mad things all this time, sat down again very sadly and quietly, and looked at Alice.

"It must be a very pretty dance," said Alice timidly.

"Would you like to see a little of it?" said the Mock Turtle.

"Very much indeed," said Alice.

"Come, let's try the first figure!" said the Mock Turtle to the Gryphon, "we can do it without lobsters, you know. Which shall sing?"

"Oh! you sing!" said the Gryphon,
"I've forgotten the words."

So they began solemnly dancing 'round
and round Alice,
every now and
then treading on
her toes when they
came too close,
and waving their
fore-paws to mark
the time, while the
Mock Turtle sang,
slowly and sadly,
these words:

"Beneath the waters of the sea
Are lobsters thick as thick can be—
They love to dance with you and me,
My own, my gentle Salmon!"

The Gryphon joined in singing the chorus,
which was:

"Salmon come up! Salmon go down!
Salmon come twist your tail around!
Of all the fishes of the sea
There's none so good as Salmon!"

"Thank you," said Alice, feeling very glad that the figure was over.

"Shall we try the second figure?" said the Gryphon, "or would you prefer a song?"

"Oh, a song, please!" Alice replied, so eagerly, that the Gryphon said, in a rather offended tone, "hm! no accounting for tastes! Sing her 'Mock Turtle Soup', will you, old fellow!"

The Mock Turtle sighed deeply, and began, in a voice sometimes choked with sobs, to sing this:

"Beautiful Soup, so rich and green,
    Waiting in a hot tureen!
Who for such dainties would not stoop?
Soup of the evening, beautiful Soup!
Soup of the evening, beautiful Soup!
        Beau — ootiful Soo — oop!
        Beau — ootiful Soo - oop!
    Soo - oop of the e - e - evening,
        Beautiful beautiful Soup!

"Chorus again!" cried the Gryphon, and

the Mock Turtle had just begun to repeat it, when a cry of "the trial's beginning!" was heard in the distance.

"Come on!" cried the Gryphon, and, taking Alice by the hand, he hurried off, without waiting for the end of the song.

"What trial is it?" panted Alice as she ran, but the Gryphon only answered "come on!" and ran the faster, and more and more faintly came, borne on the breeze that followed them, the melancholy words:

"Soo—oop of the e—e—evening,
Beautiful beautiful Soup!"

The King and Queen were seated on their throne when they arrived, with a great crowd assembled around them: the Knave was in custody: and before the King stood the white rabbit, with a trumpet in one hand, and a scroll of parchment in the other.

"Herald! read the accusation!" said the King.

On this the white rabbit blew three blasts on the trumpet, and then unrolled the parchment scroll, and read as follows:

"The Queen of Hearts she made some tarts
     All on a summer day:
The Knave of Hearts he stole those tarts,
     And took them quite away!"

"Now for the evidence," said the King, "and then the sentence."

"No!" said the Queen, "first the sentence, and then the evidence!"

"Nonsense!" cried Alice, so loudly that everybody jumped, "the idea of having the sentence first!

"Hold your tongue!" said the Queen.

"I won't!" said Alice, "you're nothing but a pack of cards! Who cares for you?"

At this the whole pack rose up into the air, and came flying down upon her: she gave a little scream of fright, and tried to beat them off, and found herself lying on the bank, with her head in the lap of her sister, who was gently brushing away some leaves that had fluttered down from the trees on to her face.

"Wake up, Alice dear!" said her sister, "what a nice long sleep you've had!"

"Oh, I've had such a curious dream!" said Alice, and she told her sister all her Adventures Under Ground, as you have read them, and when she had finished, her sister kissed her and said "it _was_ a curious dream, dear, certainly! But now run in to your tea : it's getting late."

So Alice ran off, thinking while she ran (as well she might) what a wonderful dream it had been.

But her sister sat there some while longer, watching the setting sun, and thinking of little Alice and her Adventures, till she too began dreaming after a fashion, and this was her dream:

She saw an ancient city, and a quiet river winding near it along the plain, and up the stream went slowly gliding a boat with a merry party of children on board — she could hear their voices and laughter like music over the water — and among them was another little Alice, who sat listening with bright eager eyes to a tale that was being told, and she listened for the words of the tale, and lo! it was the dream of her own little sister. So the boat wound slowly along, beneath the bright summer-day, with its merry crew and its music of voices and laughter, till it passed round one of the many turnings of the stream, and she saw it no more.

Then she thought, (in a dream within the dream, as it were,) how this same little Alice would, in the after-time, be herself a grown woman: and how she would keep, through her riper years, the simple and loving heart of her childhood: and how she would gather around her other little children, and make their eyes bright and eager with many a wonderful tale, perhaps even with these very adventures of the little Alice of long-ago: and how she would feel with all their simple sorrows, and find a pleasure in all their simple joys, remembering her own child-life, and the happy summer-days.

First published as a facsimile reproduction by
The Folio Society 2008

This edition first published 2008 by
The British Library
96 Euston Road
London NW1 2DB

Reprinted with new jacket 2014

Text © The British Library Board
Images © The British Library Board
and other named copyright holders

British Library Cataloguing in Publication Data
A CIP record for this volume is available
from the British Library

ISBN 978 0 7123 5600 8

Jacket design by Maggi Smith, Sixism
Typeset by Bobby Birchall

Printed in Hong Kong by Great Wall Printing Co. Ltd